IT'S NOT ME, IT'S YOU!

Rosie La Rosa

First published by Busybird Publishing 2022

Paperback: 978-1-922954-01-5

Ebook: 978-1-922954-02-2

Cover design: Kev Howlett

Layout and typesetting: Busybird Publishing

Busybird Publishing
2/118 Para Road
Montmorency, Victoria
Australia 3094
www.busybird.com.au

*This book was inspired by and dedicated
to my husband and children
who have been
a never-ending source of support and love.*

Disclaimer

This book is a satire, an amalgamation of stories of fictitious characters based on behaviours observed through all walks of life.

Each chapter has been created based on these characteristics with a touch of embellishment.

It also serves as a mirror to those individuals who continue to behave badly and treat others with disrespect.

To those people I say, 'Although others have not held you accountable, I see you and your behaviour is not okay.'

INTRODUCTION

People are interesting beings.

The human brain is a complex system. It is believed to be compiled of over 86 billion neurons. Add to this the influences of nature and nurture, which also contribute to human behaviour. Endeavouring to understand some people can prove futile.

Some organisations will use the assistance of a psychometric test to measure a candidate's suitability for a role

These tests evaluate four main categories:

- aptitude
- personality
- behaviours, and
- emotional intelligence.

To gain a holistic perspective of the candidate's suitability, a psychometric test should be used as part of the recruitment process together with an interview.

Most people have a predominant tendency and fit nicely into a particular category – a great way to identify behaviours, leadership qualities, and general intelligence.

Some people, however, demand a new category all to themselves.

These are the people that we meet every day. They leave you feeling flummoxed and confused.

When it comes to them, I have come realise …

It's NOT me. It's you!

THE SMILEY SPIDER

The Smiley Spider appears to be lovely.

She is softly spoken and has a calm nature about her, almost too good to be true.

When something appears too good to be true it usually is.

Her smiley calm nature is what will draw you into her strategically placed web. Anyone outside of her web only sees this lovely side, but those captured see another side.

The passive aggressive side.

The Smiley Spider is very clever about how she will reveal this side, stunning and catching her unsuspecting prey when they least expect it. She spins her web and pierces her prey with her fangs, injecting them with a neurotoxin to ensure paralysis.

Then the strike!

She undermines her prey in work meetings, with an audience, so that the impact creates maximum carnage.

Raising awareness of the Smiley Spider's antics to the powers-that- be is of no use. They do not see past her softly spoken demeanour. Anyone flagging such behaviours is seen as an instigator because Smiley Spider is so sweet.

Working within a web is incredibly difficult. You are stuck to the thread that you landed on, making any task now seem impossible. It is like trying to complete any tasks with one arm tied behind your back.

The only way out of the web is to escape when the Spider is distracted.

This is no easy feat.

The web is incredibly strong and the prey soon learns that the more they struggle the more tangled they become.

Taking a calm and calculated approach, the prey waits for an opportune time to break free, leave and move on.

Smiley Spider stays close to her web and continues to smile at the right people in the right circles. She continues to portray the image of a sweet natured, calm, and softly spoken person – just lovely.

No one is even noticing the shaking coming from the web from the newly captured prey.

LITTLE LUCY

Lucy lives in a quant quiet suburb with her migrant parents and two older brothers. The house she grew up in appears to be a standard weatherboard from the front, but behind the façade lies a secret that she wants to keep – an enormous vegetable garden sprawled across more than half of the yard, and tucked away in the back, a shed.

But this is no ordinary shed. No lawn mower or tools in sight. Cupboards and benchtops discarded by others have been thrown together to form a patchwork kitchen.

It's a hub of activity where Lucy and her brothers are raised among traditional Italian cooking. Strong smells of garlic from the large pot of pasta sauce, and the frying of schnitzels and homemade hot chips permeate the walls and Lucy's existence.

Such a tiny space would host numerous meals extended to cousins, aunts, grandparents and neighbourhood friends but Lucy wants to keep the shed a secret that she only divulges to a select few.

Waiting by the front brick fence, Lucy's friends arrive, and together they walk to school.

Somewhere along the way Lucy would reach into her bag and grab her prepacked lunch which her father had prepared the night before. It consists of whatever's left over from dinner packed into two roughly cut slices of pasta dura bread.

Lucy keeps the apple and the small box of sultanas – these items are considered normal – and throws away the large smelly sandwich. Lucy's so skilled that her friends never witness the sandwich flying through the air and landing in a stranger's front yard.

Her house is for sleeping and bathing and nothing else. It is kept in a clean, dustless, almost museum-like state and although the loungeroom does contain a baroque couch, Lucy is thankful that it does not have a protective plastic sheet over it.

Summers are spent in the shed watching an old and very small television unit and harvesting all the vegetables that her father grows in his veggie patch. Lucy and her brothers sit and shell beans, separating them by colour and bagging them into freezer bags.

Just when they finish the recently picked harvest, Lucy's dad comes in with another large box ready for shelling. This process goes on for hours, until Lucy decides that they have had enough.

She has a plan.

She places a handwritten sign on the door which simply reads BEAN STRIKE! Her dad gives a rare half smile but proceeds to place another full box of beans in the middle of the table.

Lucy hates the shed. She knows that her friends live their lives in houses and that she is different – until her teenage years, when Lucy realises that the shed is a space to hang with her friends and, eventually, a boyfriend. Her parents go to bed early so the shed becomes a place to chill, watch TV loudly, eat snacks and drink coffee.

As Lucy is the youngest, she is the remote control, turning the clunky knob of television and hoping that one of the three channels will have something funny to watch.

Looking back, Lucy realises times spent in that cramped old shed with her brothers, laughing, eating, hanging with friends, and watching reruns of her favourite shows, was a place of warmth, love, family, and friends.

As an adult, Lucy lives in a house where all the cooking is prepared in the kitchen. Her teenage children are exposed to the shed-way of life via the grandparents.

Although her parents moved house, they ensured they had a shed in the yard with a kitchen and a massive table.

Lucy enjoys the many family meals and celebrations in the new shed, loud and cramped but surrounded by laughter and copious amounts of home-cooked meals

But she also looks forward to returning to her own home, her arms loaded up with leftover food to be stored in the fridge and ready to be reheated in her house-based kitchen.

Yes, Chef!

N ever have I ever met such a character.

She is almost of retirement age and has been at the same organisation her entire working life. She has a routine, the same one that has been in play from the very beginning – the same menu on offer.

She has a hard, angry face and she rarely smiles. No warmth. She prepares the daily meals in the domain of her kitchen.

No one is to be walking through the kitchen, no one talking near the kitchen and there are to be no interruptions while she prepares the same meals she has prepared repeatedly for years on end.

She is not open to feedback on her menu or routine – even the slightest change. Better options are not welcome.

Quizzed about why she uses powdered milk to make milkshakes? Fresh milk would seem a better option – surely this is obvious.

The Chef scoffs that she has always used powdered milk to make milkshakes. The mere suggestion of fresh milk enrages the Chef. Her scowl could kill.

Hiding behind the excuse that powdered milk is cheaper and that the budget does not allow for fresh milk, she simply refuses to change. Any change is seen as relinquishing power and she will not do that.

After more than twenty years, the Chef retires. She takes her menu, her routine and her anger with her. She is farewelled with a lovely celebration for her years of service and dedication. She is given a parting gift of flowers and a cake made with real flour and is wished a happy retirement. She will be missed as much as the powdered milk.

The staff are now free to walk and talk past and through the kitchen, which was previously a no-go zone.

The new chef enjoys the company of the other staff and even shares a laugh or two. Taking stock of the pantry, the new chef discards items that she intends to replace with fresher ingredients. Discarded items include powdered milk, tinned soup, tinned vegetables and tinned spaghetti, just to name a few.

The new chef discusses the budget and amendments to the menu that include a weekly supply of fresh milk.

The new weekly menu on display is reviewed and changed frequently, enticing fragrances wafting through the hallway and greeting all.

A happier place all round.

A monotonous routine no more.

Angry chef be gone, discarded unceremoniously, along with the packets of powdered milk trashed in the dumpster.

Unassuming Artist

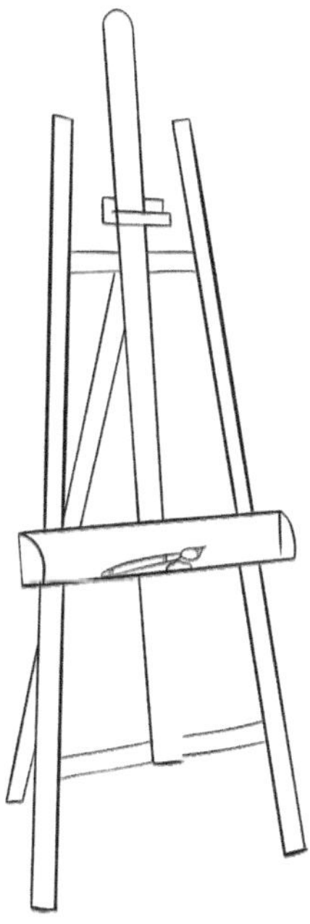

She is born and raised on a rural property with cows, sheep, horses, chickens and two adorable Border Collies and with not a lot to do. Spare time is spent learning to play the piano and creating things, building things, tinkering away in her dad's large farm shed. Surrounded by dust, rusty tools, a snake or two and hundreds of spiders, she is at home.

One of six children, she fights for everything – attention from her parents, food, clothing. She learns quickly that she can command attention through her quick-witted humour.

She joins a teenage band and although she is not the lead singer, she has a stage presence that cannot be denied. Coupled with her natural beauty and cascading long flowing hair, she soon develops a following of adoring fans. A country girl at heart she enjoys the attention but does not let it go to her head.

Her first serious relationship is with a man who accepts her for all that she is: funny, quirky, beautiful, a talented musician, a country girl at heart and an all-round good person. The relationship inevitably leads to marriage. He is gentle, patient, loving and just as talented.

For years, she works as an art lecturer at the local university while still playing in a band on the weekend and tinkering away in her tin shed in her spare time. The couple have two adorable children – a boy and a girl – and build their dream home. It has a large shed.

Time for a change, she opens her own very small art school providing intimate workshops. This new venture provides the perfect opportunity for her to indulge in her creativity whilst still be able to partake in all her other pastimes. She revels in all of her roles – especially being a loving wife and mother.

During an art class she discovers that she has created a unique and original sculpture. Unlike anything else, she has a name for the piece and a story as to how it came to be. The piece is inspired by a time in her life and is now a stunning creation.

The sculpture introduces a new artist to the world. Tinkering away, she creates a series of pieces. Each has a name and backstory for its creation. No two pieces are the same.

The collection is proudly on display in a local exhibition. Each piece is placed in a museum with strategic lighting. Gaining momentum, the exhibitions appear on the local evening news and in local newspapers.

As the first sculpture sells, she takes a breath and realises she is now a creator, an artist. She retreats to her art class to tinker away and allows inspiration to take over and creates her next masterpiece.

She is the unassuming artist.

The Storm

The Storm can only be described as a human storm cloud – a tall presence of a man extremely unhappy with his life. He lives perpetually in an *oh woe is me* state of mind.

A storm can occur anywhere at any time. It may bring destructive winds, flash flooding, bruising hailstones and searing lightning. Storm damage can vary from broken branches to cracked tiles to smashed windows.

In this storm you are not allowed to be happy. You must endure the lightning and thunder that follows him like a grey cloud looming around his head. Hear his thunder! Witness his lightning strike anyone in his path.

Only the Storm can have an opinion on anything. You shall not have an opinion of your own.

Shocks can be felt for miles. So much so that even Management will stay away from the Storm for fear of being struck.

The Storm conducts himself in an unprofessional manner, grumbling his way through each day and doing whatever he pleases.

It is important to be aware of the dangers of such severe weather and what you can do to protect yourself. Evacuate if you feel it is your best line of defence. Clear a path to the door and pack essential supplies in your bag. When the path is clear make a run for it.

Go.

Run.

This Storm has not blown over for years and is forecast to remain for years to come.

Monitor weather warnings and stay out of the eye of the Storm.

You have been warned.

A Beautiful Mind

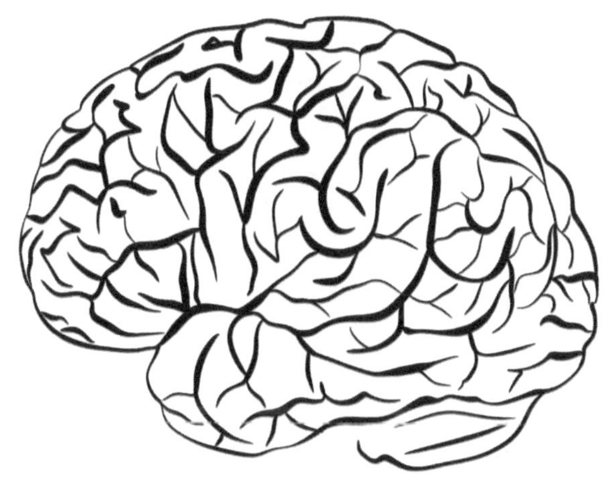

He is a control freak as much as he is brilliant. Most people will either have book smarts or street smarts, but rarely do you encounter this wonderful species: highly educated, self-motivated and driven, he has both.

His brain shall be donated to science when he passes to study and dissect and endeavour to understand this intriguing creature.

His logical mindset and thinking mean that he will not suffer fools lightly. He will give you his opinion regardless of whether you asked for it.

Even with meaningless tasks, he feels the need to tell you a better way of doing things. The better way is always his way. Frustrating at times, but he is always right.

Being told that everything you do can and should be done better does not sit well with some people. They challenge him, stand still and continue to perform the task at hand in the manner they want. After all, the task will be done. Does it really matter how? He would argue, 'Yes.' If it is worth doing, it is worth doing well.

His brain is like the mechanics of an industrial switchboard, an array of colours and bright lights all twinkling purposefully. This switchboard never rests. Ideas are created here and nurtured in the realm of thought.

Once an idea is generated, he is hellbent on bringing it to life. All blockers that would deter anyone else are seen as a challenge. Each challenge is faced front on.

'I shall and will get you not only to see things my way but clear the path that leads to fruition.'

Every angle is visited and studied – each with its own set of pros and cons – and when all of the angles are investigated to the nth degree, he strikes.

He is despised by many who only see him as bold or too controlling. Others are envious of his rare, beautiful mind and in awe of his ability to ration and achieve even the most unachievable.

A tough exterior but squishy inside, he loves with all that he is. Many have admired by afar but few have seen firsthand the lengths he will go to help someone he loves.

If you are lucky enough to be in his inner circle hold onto that diamond. What you have is priceless! Even if the chewing is too loud and the breathing reminds you of a bull.

He is a wealth of knowledge, experience, and common sense. Drives all around him batty and yet they are all the better for having him around.

PROTECTED SPECIES

F ear the person in power or friends with someone in power.

The Protected Species is both.

Her office is located within proximity of the CEO – in fact, she is within earshot. They are close friends and are often spotted out for dinners and drinks and always sitting together in the staff room for endless chats and cups of tea.

This Protected Species has a quite a presence about her. Openly rude, she walks past staff without any acknowledgement, deeming them beneath her.

No hello.

No side glances.

No slight smile.

Her remarks are fast, almost whiplike, leaving the unsuspecting victim to contemplate what just happened.

Proud of the fact that she treats others badly, she tells stories of the many staff who reported her behaviour – official complaints of bullying to the organisation.

But, in the end, they would always leave. She says this like it is an achievement, something to strive for, and she wears her bad behaviour like a badge of honour.

It is an employer's responsibility to keep all employees safe. The organisation has a policy stating that it provides a safe and respectful workplace. It details what constitutes bullying, be it verbal or in via email. Bullying will not be tolerated.

The policy sits on the bookshelf, collecting dust.

Not one to hide her behaviours, the Protected Species thrives on having an audience to witness them. Others leave her presence upset, in tears and scarred by her sharp tongue. They are dismayed the behaviour was observed, heard by management, but not addressed

She openly delegates unachievable tasks to the same few staff every time. She ensures that her friends were spared any additional tasks. She does this often. Openly. Witnessed by all.

Management having witnessed the behaviour still choose to ignore it, making excuses.

'She doesn't mean anything by it.'

'She is very busy.'

'Her knee is giving her a lot of grief.'

'Her cat is unwell.'

'It was a joke.'

'When you get to know her, you will banter back.'

There is a section of the policy that states management must understand what bullying is, know how to prevent it and to take prompt action to address it.

Having the courage to raise the behaviour with management is a daunting thought, though many have tried. They are always met with the same excuses. Wait! What? Really? The excuses for her behaviour and the bullying need to stop.

The Employee Assistance Program, EAP, upon hearing countless ways in which staff were being treated, and that management did nothing to address the behaviour advised the only way they could: 'Make an exit plan and get out of there.'

End of year social function and the drinks are flowing with chatter and good cheer all round. Under the influence of the truth serum the joke is told: 'We all know Protected Species is a total bitch.'

The entire staff share a nervous giggle but are all thinking the same thing: *You know about this and not only are you not addressing it, but you are also giving her permission to continue to do so.*

The sad truth is that she is and always will be a protected species.

NEW LEASE

Married for many years, a good life and a good marriage. Three children together, now grown and adulting on their own, and she has a big birthday around the corner.

Taking stock, she ticks off the boxes.

Raised children?

Check.

Cooked and kept house?

Check.

Been a loving and devoted wife?

Check.

Achieved any of her own goals?

…?

Not able to check that box, the list starts to unravel in her head and grows.

What now?

A big question mark looms over her head. She feels present in the real world, but nobody sees her, nobody hears her screaming.

Finally, she breaks the sound barrier. This BOOM is the deafening sound of the revelation that she will now put herself first.

Everyone stops what they are doing, and they look closely. At first glance what they see is the same person.

But upon closer inspection they can see she is different. She has a new purpose! A new lease on life.

Her stance is strong and confident. She starts to check off items from her list one by one. There are some she cannot check off. She wants to, but in order to do that she needs to cut old ties that are holding her back. Something has to give. The marriage must give.

Flying solo opens a whole new world. It is all very exciting. New places to see, new people to meet, new wardrobe, new home, new tattoos.

New! New! New!

Making way for new is letting go of the old. Not easy to say goodbye to some of the old but necessary to make way for the new.

Now for all to know that the New Lease has arrived. Smiles for miles and different scenery paint a picture that the grass is greener on the other side. Seemingly so green, sparkling like an emerald that dazzles all who see it.

But if you look closely, if you look through the glamour you will see the blades of brown. They have been, filtered and sprayed over to hide the not-so-perfect truth.

THE RUNNER UP

The Runner Up has been acting in the role of manager for a few months now and the committee decides to advertise the role. The Runner Up applies but is unsuccessful in her application. An external applicant is appointed, and the Runner Up is relegated back to her position of second in charge.

Some people will be okay with this and understand the interview process was an opportunity for the best candidate for the role while others will take it personally and then apply underhanded tactics in an attempt to undermine the newly appointed manager.

When presented with the option to take the moral high road or behave poorly, the Runner Up naturally chooses the second option.

She attempts to employ a gang mentality, a majority rule line of defence. She spends her time preparing PowerPoint presentations and sales pitches to deliver to the other team members and enlist them on her side.

The New Manager, oblivious to the antics of the Runner Up, goes about her day. Every time she is absent, the Runner Up tells the others all the perceived ways that the new manager is 'failing' at the role. She builds what she believes to be a body of evidence to be used against the New Manager at the upcoming committee meeting.

What she doesn't count on is not everyone is sold on THE PLAN. One staff member does not agree with the Runner Up's underhanded nature and decides to meet with the unsuspecting New Manager to fill her in on THE PLAN. Although it's not what the New Manager is expecting to hear, she is also a little amused.

Armed with THE PLAN, the New Manager informs the committee.

On the night of the meeting the committee give the floor to the Runner Up and the staff who are onboard with THE PLAN.

They feel empowered, like they are fighting for justice, however delusional. They feel they have been heard and vindicated, certain that they will achieve the desired outcome of the committee firing the New Manager. After all, they have been rehearsing this sales pitch for a while and mastered the delivery.

The Runner Up speaks. A sly smile on her face and knowing glances to the others, eyes darting back and forth, she sits down to hear the response from the committee, eagerly awaiting the firing of the manager.

The committee ask if they have finished. They proceed to tell the staff that not only are they more than happy with the performance of the New Manager, but she is here to stay. Furthermore, if they are not happy with this decision, they are free to hand in their resignations.

The sly smiles are no more.

The months that follow are filled with self-sabotaging behaviour. The Runner Up continues to break regulations, placing the lives of others at risk. The staff who she recruited are now informing the New Manager of such behaviours and a work performance case is beginning to grow.

A meeting is held to address these matters and a verbal warning issued. The Runner Up leaves the meeting in tears, screaming she would not be back on Monday.

The Committee and the New Manager say, 'We should have got that in writing.'

Monday morning, however, she is back and with a new union membership in hand.

The Runner Up continues to behave in an unprofessional manner – sick days on a Monday as she is too drunk from her partying over the weekend.

Her stories of weekend liaisons and dalliances are too much to bear for the other staff. She shares the most intimate and graphic details to whomever is in earshot, regardless of if they want to listen.

The Runner Up leaves eventually but not before trying to sue the organisation for unfair dismissal, even though she handed in her resignation.

THE ASSEMBLY

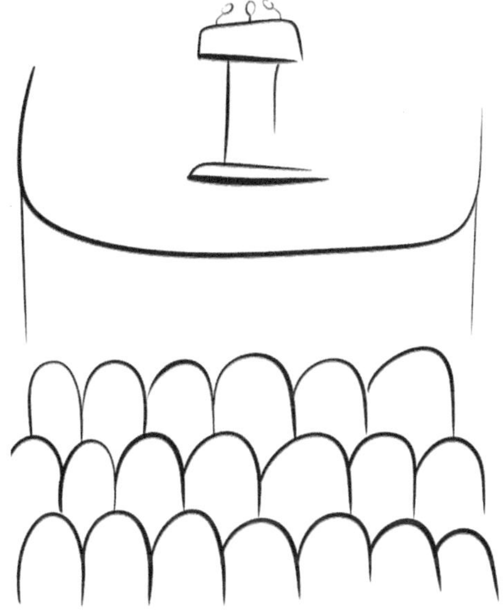

The Assembly has a charismatic leader with teachings of upmost importance. Members are discouraged from questioning and are required to conform. Outsiders are classified as non-believers.

New members are love bombed, lured into the welcoming folds with smiles and fun social activities – laughter, a glass of bubbly and lots of commonalities. You think, *Well, this is so much fun and so easy.* This is a deliberate practice to foster a sense of belonging.

When in the presence of this group they make you feel important, needed and that you are home. It must be real! Look at how much emotion and affirmations are coming your way. Why was I doubting this?

Communication from hereon is generic. Your presence is required to attend the upcoming gathering where you are pitched an out-of-this-world, pure-life experience. Join the enthusiasts, attend weekly meetings where multiple donations are collected to ensure longevity of the group.

Those introducing new members are celebrated and awarded with the important task of addressing the masses. The more people who join, the more successful the group.

You feel yourself sliding out of the conscience sales pitch that is directed at all in the room. Your thoughts start to run wild.

What is happening right now?

Does everyone believe what they are saying?

And if so, why?

How do I get them to snap out of this trance-like hold?

But stop and look.

Look closely and you will see. They are singing the songs with gusto. Yes, they believe, they have been sold the pitch and are now preaching the word to the non-believer.

The realisation hits you hard, what is being pitched is not for you.

Taking a step back and shaking off the Assembly you return to your life in the land of the non-believer.

The Dinosaur

The Dinosaur has been in the same job since the Jurassic Period 200 million years ago. Although she has never progressed, changed roles or upskilled, she feels entitled to be the unofficial manager.

Believing that she is, she calls the shots from the sidelines by whispering to others after meetings and undermining any new changes or improvements.

The modern-day rules do not apply to her. They never have so why would they now? She comes and goes as she pleases and runs her own show.

Part of a team? Nope! The Dinosaur is happy to roam her natural habitat and stomps on the same terrain that she stomped on the day before. Don't ask the Dinosaur to change her routine or learn anything new. She will tell you that she already knows this anyway.

Some might say the Dinosaur has millions of years' experience, but does she really? Or is it one year's experience repeated over and over? It's interesting that some might see this as a positive, that the Dinosaur can stay in its habitat for so long without change.

Year in, year out.

Decade in and out.

Anyone new coming into this habitat is seen as a Rookie. You are green and must prove yourself. Not prove yourself with your experience and qualifications – no. You must prove yourself by standing with the Dinosaur and stomping the same terrain. Your ability to adapt and behave like a Baby Dino is your initiation, even if you are the Dinosaur's leader.

You are in a constant state of performance as your survival depends on your acting skills. Most Actors will fail as they grow tired of the façade. They want to achieve and progress but the Dinosaur stomps, roars and blocks all attempts for improvement.

When the actor sheds the Baby Dino suit, the performance will end. The curtains will be drawn and the actor will breathe a sigh of relief as they exit the Jurassic Period to re-enter the modern world.

The Dinosaur stomps away back over the same tracks, the earth shuddering under each step.

SUNSHINE

S he is tall but that is not what you notice when you
first meet her. It is that she is friendly and bubbly and
full of life! She feels like sunshine walking into the room.

Her long legs give her a clumsy quality that add to
her endearing personality. She shoots sunrays without
even knowing it and lights up the life of all she touches.
She is ever happy, ever content with an enormous heart
full of compassion, care and kindness.

Sunshine devotes her energy into illuminating others.
She knows that she has this magical healing power. She
doesn't know why but she tries desperately to save
every lost soul that is slowly dimming.

Her healing rays provide love, food, care, and a
shoulder to cry on, without a thought for her own bright
light. She gives so much of herself that she doesn't notice
her own illumination being deliberately drained by the
ever-needy self-absorbed.

Powers fading, sad and scared, Sunshine takes
some much-needed solace. She rests under the security
blanket of love provided by her elders.

Some are unaware they are draining her while others
are more calculated. The world is now dull without her
beautiful luminous rays spreading happiness.

Faces reflect the same shade of grey with moods to match. A select few see this time as their time to shine and revel in the knowledge that Sunshine has been dimmed.

The blanket of love continues to provide a layer of comfort, support and protection, shielding Sunshine from the devious few. The shield offers more than a barrier of impenetrable protection – it offers Sunshine a sense of belonging.

I am loved.

I am appreciated.

I am safe.

Rested, refuelled and with a full tank, Sunshine sets out to spread her healing rays far and wide.

Knowing not all that she encounters are worthy of her healing rays, Sunshine remains true to who she is. She continues to beam her rays in areas of darkness.

For now, the blanket is folded neatly and placed safely on a shelf.

If you know someone who feels like Sunshine, do not let them go. They are a rare breed. And you are incredibly lucky!

THE LEECH

A leech has two definitions – a bloodsucking parasite and a person who sponges off others.

This Leech could add a third definition to the dictionary: they suck the life out of you in every way possible.

The Leech will befriend you and have you believe that they care about you as much as you care about them. For a while, things are great and you are included in important functions and events and because you are friends you do what you can to support them.

While things are good you cannot see the damage that the Leech is doing as they suck the life out of you at such a slow but steady pace that you don't even notice.

They'll leech time, calling you at all hours and complaining about the woes of life. The phone calls go for hours, and the conversation is a monologue where you are not allowed to have thoughts or feelings. Your sole purpose is to be the sponge that absorbs all of the negativity until The Leech feels better and you end up with a splitting headache. You are now carrying the burdens bestowed upon you by the Leech.

Your home gets infested too! The Leech thinks nothing of coming over all the time – not for a quick chat or visit. Oh no! They park in the driveway and settle in for lunch, followed by afternoon tea, multiple cuppas and then dinner, of course. If you're lucky, you might have an hour to yourself before the end of the weekend – well, after serving the leech hand and foot for hours on end of course.

At times the Leech needs financial support and you think nothing of it. After all, you think they care about you as much as you care about them.

The Leech takes your time, money, food, house, emotions and completely sucks you dry.

When you no longer serve a purpose the Leech creates a reason that only they could possibly believe to throw you away. Just like that! You have been depleted of everything.

What remains is an empty shell.

That shell is now sharper and wiser and can spot a Leech from miles away.

Should a Leech sneak past the line of defence copious bags of salt are stockpiled in the pantry.

Ready for use.

Doormat

An open heart worn on her sleeve, she is an easy target. Being herself, she gives her all. New friendships come easily and connections are formed. Light-hearted texts and giggles are a daily occurrence. Social events are inevitable, and Doormat happily coordinates the group for dinners, movies and drinks. She plans everything so that the event is fun, but others are non-committal.

'Oh maybe, I'll see how I go.'

To her face they are nice, and they act like they care about her and maybe they do on some level but as soon as she is out of sight she is definitely out of mind.

Overlooked and undervalued she is left out of things openly. With hurt setting in and the realisation that perhaps she values the friendships more than they do, she crawls back into her head, into her shell, into herself.

When anyone else arranges a night out the others are all on board. No second guessing. No excuses. Just all in. Doormat joins the conversation and of course she will go. Then the in-jokes continue and Doormat is once again overlooked and left out. Back into her shell she goes.

Doormat does her best to get on with things and forms another friendship. It's new and fresh and feels light-hearted and fun. They share laughs, texts, commonalities and she enjoys feeling valued. It feels genuine.

Once again, she goes all in, coordinates fun events and initially the friend happily accepts until the excuses start and the pattern repeat.

Back into the shell Doormat goes.

She does not know why this happens to her – if people mistake her kindness for weakness, and thus take advantage of her. Or because these people are snide. There is only confusion.

Being a Doormat has a taken a toll. The horsehair is no longer standing tall and has been squished and compacted from all the foot traffic. She is not the same, not willing to easily let anyone else in.

Guarded and armed with the wisdom that only hurt can provide, she transforms into a stunning new tapestry. No longer will others wipe their feet on her, she is now to be curated perfectly on a wall to be admired.

A rare commodity, a genuine friend you would be lucky to have but now only available to a select few.

POLYANNA KNOW IT ALL

Outwardly she appears to always be happy and smiling and singing the praises of the organisation's righteousness. She is a manager and not afraid to use her title, even in inappropriate settings. She is tall, and her legs appear quite lanky, like an uncoordinated giraffe.

Pollyanna will always turn things around. Any matters that require guidance and advice are met with anecdotes, and fables of how much better she is at everything, even if the stories are not even remotely relevant.

You are left baffled. Confused. Walking away scratching your head, you think, *What was that?*

She professes to know all and have the answers to everything, but when challenged with correct information, she will accuse the staff member of being difficult. Then she pulls out all stops to prove her point.

She knows everything, after all.

She has jingles with her name and is not afraid to sing them loud and proud.

I am good.

I am great.

Even when things are neither good, nor great.

It is frightening when you report to someone who professes to know it all, but in reality, does not know anything.

She is a people pleaser. Pollyanna wants to be liked. *Adored.* She does her best to convince others that they, too, would benefit from being optimistic and positive even when the situation does not warrant such attitudes. She attempts to explain and justify all evils. She lives and breathes in a world of delusions whilst others live in the real world.

It is not healthy to live in a world where anything other than happiness is ignored. It is not good to sweep everything into a messy pile. Surely, there will come a time where you will trip over the ever-growing mound.

In order to fix a problem first you need to acknowledge that there is a problem. Ignoring it will only make it worse. So, too, is pretending that all is well.

Pollyanna likes to remind others that she is so good, she has been elevated to a status that no one else can possibly reach.

I am beneath her.

You are beneath her.

We are all beneath her.

She will sing her jingle and use her jazz hands to spread the word far and wide. Conversations always revert to her. Her way. Her story. Her solution.

Her.

Her.

Her.

She has no clue that the staff do their best to avoid her.

Pollyanna continues to smile at all and tell anyone nearby fables of sunshine, lollipops and rainbows.

Marshal Men

A newly created job born out of necessity in the midst of a global pandemic. Two new staff are excited to be offered shifts when many have been laid off as a result of lengthy lockdowns.

It has been a while since they have had a solid couple weeks of steady work, and they arrive with a sense of pride. Like a changing of the guards, there is one for the morning shift and the other for the afternoon.

Dressed for the part, they wear name badges on their bright uniforms. They position themselves at their post, ready to take on the new role.

They need to check eligibility of everybody walking through the doors. They are met with unhappy community members who previously could access every section of the facility without question, now needing to prove that they have a valid reason to be there.

The Marshal Men are challenged and questioned by a disgruntled few. Some hurl ugly abuse, but the Marshal Men take on the negativity with professionalism and do their best to educate the abusers about why the changes have been implemented.

Both have a calm nature and sense of humour. They face the backlash with humility. They take pride in seemingly tedious tasks, such as:

- ensuring common touch point areas are routinely sanitised.
- that furniture is rearranged to ensure restriction requirements.
- and that information is updated and displayed.

A role created for just a couple of weeks extends to a few months. They are incredibly grateful that they can able to secure a job, even an unpopular one. Accepting this role enables them some financial freedom, even if it's for a short-lived period.

They are respected and appreciated by the staff working in the building facing backlash by the same disgruntled few. It is a collective effort to work through some of the toughest conditions to manage.

Inevitably, the role comes to end as restrictions change and ease. Both remain part of a casual pool of staff called upon for an odd job here or there.

Before they finish, both express how appreciative they have been, not simply for some much-needed work but for the first time feeling valued.

Every person regardless of role or level of seniority needs to be treated with the respect. An organisation

can have countless policies on inclusivity but all that is
needed is an overarching statement.

Fair and equitable for all.

People never forget how they were treated.

Be kind always.

75

BACKSTABBER

The Backstabber is always talking about her friends – whoever isn't present for the social event is the topic of conversation.

The others listen politely. Secretly, they are hoping that she will talk about any other topic.

The Backstabber has a strong personality and no one has the courage to tell her they are uncomfortable with the conversation.

The conversation goes round and round. Seeing a break in the airtime the others jump in and discuss, families, children, upcoming plans. It works! They have achieved the goal of steering the discussion in other directions. This helps for a little while, but then the Backstabber takes the floor once again.

And we are back on.

Given the Backstabber would talk about each of her current friends, you would have to be a fool to think she would not be talking about you in your absence.

Of course, she is.

It is both sad and comical to think that the Backstabber would not realise that her friends know this.

Life should not be about who is real to your face but rather who is real behind your back. It is important to know that everybody is not your friend. Just because you hang around some people and share some laughs over a dinner does not mean they are genuinely your friend.

Read situations.

Judge for yourself.

If you feel uncomfortable, remove yourself and take comfort in solitude instead of the company of disingenuous people.

POCKET FRIENDS

Have you met those couples that make friends with other couples and before you know it they do everything together? They alternate going over to one another's house for dinner, and even holiday together.

They take annual camping trips, packing an entire house into the boot of the latest four-wheel drive and a trailer and drive out to camp . They set up family sized tents which they will call home for the next five nights.

All the while the children run around unsupervised because they are surrounded by nature. What could possibly go wrong? Each set up competes with the next tent. Bigger blow-up beds, portable closets, portable kitchens, portable house. Just add water to inflate.

They spend every waking minute together drinking beers and copious amounts of tea while the children run, shriek and scream, scaring any wildlife trying to nestle in their habitat in the hope they will not be seen. Somehow this outdoor experience bonds the two families.

They become so close that they live in each other's pockets and lock out other friends. And good on them! Why not? If they have found a couple that they absolutely gelled with, that's great.

It is almost inevitable that these pocket friends will have a falling out and before long they do. Time spent together once enjoyable is now a chore. Annoyance over the quirks of the other couple start to increase.

Always late.

Always speaking poorly of her partner.

Always controlling what activities will take place and when.

Always choosing the better camp spot.

The couple moves onto the next couple and the cycle repeats itself.

Having known them for years, you've seen this happen time and time again. Couple after couple. Same story just different names. It's a pattern of behaviour that is self-perpetuating.

And when the pocket friends are no more it is always the fault of the other couple.

Always!

WORK FUNCTIONS

I t is your turn to organise works next social function. Coordinating the day to suit all is no easy feat. Some respond and others do not. Planning for the function proves to be harder than it should be.

To simply choose one restaurant without exhaustively considering the menu would not suit all as many have varied dietary requirements. With no way of knowing how many will attend, you do your best and find a restaurant with options for most dietary requirements. *Phew!* Okay the pressure is off.

Or so it would seem.

The RSVPs roll in for days leading up to the event, including the very morning of. With each one comes a new request, a new dietary requirement, a preference for another venue, preference for an alternate day or time and questions around bringing others to the team lunch.

You do your best to accommodate all the belated requests. After multiple calls to the restaurant to add even more special requests – including new guests – the event rolls around.

Everyone arrives at their own pace, some slightly early and others late, strolling in with no consideration for the others who arrived at the said time. Waiting patiently for the latecomers to arrive before ordering.

The issue of seating becomes the next challenge. Certain people not wanting to sit next to others speaks volumes. Sly squinty looks and stares dart across the table. The waitstaff arrive to commence taking orders, but the calm is short-lived as the latecomers order first.

Small talk now takes place in subgroups across the very long table. Individual discussions confirm the unspoken truth of workplace alliances. Drinks arrive first and the mood becomes jovial with pleasantries now extended further than each immediate subgroup. The meals are served – food for all dietary requirements – although not to the satisfaction of some.

Given the choice socially, some in the collective group would not choose to be friends, but as colleagues they are bound by the signed codes of conduct.

The waitstaff arrive to take coffee orders, which are as complicated as the meal requirements – powdered or leafed chai lattes, short blacks, macchiatos, piccolos, lattes with low fat, full fat, soy, almond, lactose free, extra hot, small, medium or mug.

The list goes on.

Conversation now flows freely, raucous laughter bounces off the four walls.

The bill arrives and the focus shifts onto phone calculators – the activity of number crunching to cover their own expenses. This process takes time to work through.

You're responsible for collecting the cash and lumped with the painful task of ensuring that all costs are covered. Once that is done, you walk to the cashier to pay for the meals.

Goodbyes and awkward 'Thank you for organising the lunch' pleasantries are exchanged.

Exhausted, you breathe a sigh of relief.

With a takeaway coffee in hand, you make your way back to the office to finish the day, glad that the next work event will be someone else's responsibility.

WOUNDED

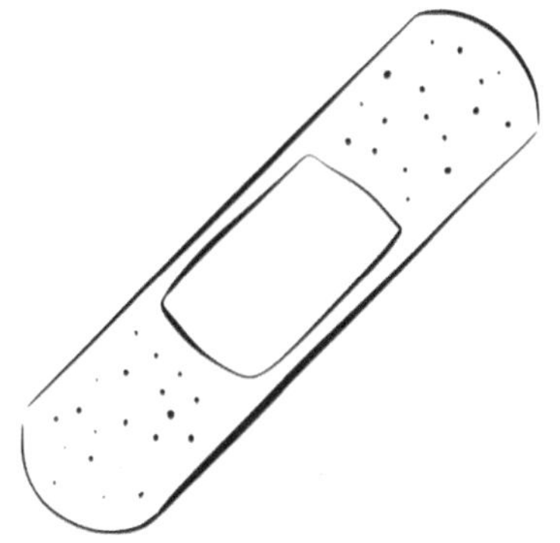

The Wounded is what remains after the explosion of a friendship.

You have been friends with her for many years – in each other's lives through everything, the good times and the bad.

When tragedy struck, the bad became a living nightmare. You made it your life's passion to support her in every way possible, even at the expense of your own relationship.

Time goes by and the level of support does not waver, not once. You are there through it all, selflessly trying to do all and provide a sense comfort. Somehow, this is not enough and you are discarded. Tossed away like garbage. No calls. No messages. Nothing!

You did not see this coming. Surely the friendship meant something? You make attempts to meet but are met with the same cold response: she is too busy, no time for you.

The realisation that the friendship is done is a hard reality to face. You question your actions. *Did I do too much? Was it not enough?* The questions remain unanswered.

You focus your time and attention elsewhere, investing in the friendships that have always been there in the background and perhaps more deserving of your time.

Interesting how the Wounded find each other. They discover that their stories are almost identical. Their pain is the same, the recovery is the same and finding each other gives them a sense of peace.

Knowing that the remaining scars have changed them forever, they are bonded by the hurt inflicted by the same person they had previously loved and trusted.

That scar remains. It is a constant reminder that you survived the hurt and grew so much that you are no longer the same person you once were.

Almost better for having gone through the hurt, you find solace in the familiarity of the other Wounded.

BUDDIES

Two work buddies – both living affected by the obsession of food.

Buddy 1 obsesses over what she will have for morning tea, lunch and snacks throughout the workday. She has a high metabolism, and obliviously burns off every calory she digests.

Buddy 2 tries desperately to conceal the fact that she is trying to survive the day on the lowest calorie count possible..

Buddy 1 has an impairment, but this does not define her. She is funny and fun! She is loud – super loud – and her laugh can be heard down the street. Her bubbly personality rubs off on all around her. Working hard, the only thing she works harder at is eating.

Buddy 2 is caring and supportive and shares a similar quirky sense of humour. Experienced and confident in her ability she supports Buddy 1 to ensure an enjoyable and productive work day. Together they take on the day's challenges and it isn't long before the focus turns to food.

Having not long consumed a large bowl of cereal for breakfast, Buddy 1 is now scouring the shelves looking for a midmorning snack to enjoy with her supersized mug of coffee.

She comes across an impressive stash of chocolates. Jackpot! A huge smile on her face, she quickly selects a couple of her favourite treats and promptly offers a sugary treat to Buddy 2. Fighting the urge, but in an attempt to conceal her restricted diet, she accepts the chocolate. With no eyes on her, she quickly hides the treat in a drawer. Out of sight, out of mind.

Not even an hour later, Buddy 1 is eating her lunch and soon ingests a second lunch. Afternoon tea is just around the corner and just when you think she has had her fair share she couldn't fit another thing in she has snacks sprinkled throughout the day. Her snacks are monster-sized bags of potato chips. And coffee. Copious amounts of coffee! When she is not eating, she is guaranteed to be thinking about eating.

Buddy 2 does her best to keep busy – too busy to stop and eat. Well, that is her excuse anyway.

The only other thing Buddy 1 loves more than eating is her love for horror movies and all things paranormal.

The buddies spend the days working hard and although they work hard they laugh a lot.

They believe the workplace has had a colourful history and have witnessed things.

Questionable things.

Things that cannot be explained.

Lights that flicker on and off, words coming from air vents, a dark shadow walking the hallway, and the TV that turns on by itself at the loudest volume.

With Buddy 1 chewing on whatever snacks she can get her hands on, and Buddy 2 fighting the familiar urge not to eat even a morsel, they exchange the most recent experiences – doors which open on their own, oven knobs turning, lights dancing during a power outage, and an animalistic growl at the end of a long narrow corridor.

Occurrences are now becoming a daily event. They engage in the services of a negative energy removal company.

They are advised to burn candles with a sweet scent at regular intervals and incense sticks to attract positive energy. Any old or broken items are discarded, and they perform white sage burning in each room.

Some time passes with no activity, and they think the cleansing must have been successful. Busily working away, they take a quick break for a cuppa, and out of the corner of their eyes they see a dark grey shadow walking down the corridor. Momentarily frozen, they look at each other and share a frightened laugh.

In the presence of such a positive, role model, Buddy 2 has finally faced more than just some dark forces within the walls of the workplace.

She has identified the one within.

She acknowledges that she needs to seek support to address her unhealthy obsession of severely restricting her food intake.

Friendship found in stress, in paranormal activity, in food – lots and lots of food – and in coffee.

These buddies are friends for life.

Red Flags

Beware the Red Flag!

She'll seem to connect with you when she sees you at drop-offs and pick-ups. She'll chat and joke and laugh with you, just like a real friend would. You connect over the fact that you find the same things funny – things that others would not.

After only a few months the friendship grows and before long you are texting daily and sending funny memes. Catching up for coffee and a chat becomes a daily occurrence throughout the week while running around.

You organise activities at the same time so that you have more time to meet and chat and all the while red flags are appearing along the way.

She:

- has no other friends.
- does not speak to any of her family members.
- will not go out socially to events like a movie or dinner.
- holds grudges for seemingly little things.
- is incredibly judgemental of others.
- makes snide comments.

Red flags get bigger and become large hurdles, but you choose to ignore them. You get along really well. Those red flags will never affect your friendship.

Until the day comes that you can no longer ignore the red flag which is now blocking the path. She stops talking to you completely! From daily to nothing. Absolutely nothing. And you don't know why. You are left trying to put together puzzle pieces, but you cannot complete the puzzle because pieces are missing.

A friend who can throw a friendship away so easily was never really a friend to begin with. They were pretending all along.

You start to collect the red flags that appeared throughout the friendship. The more you collect the more you realise that the friendship was doomed from the beginning. If only you didn't ignore the first red flag.

Lesson learned.

Do not ignore the red flags.

PERFORMER

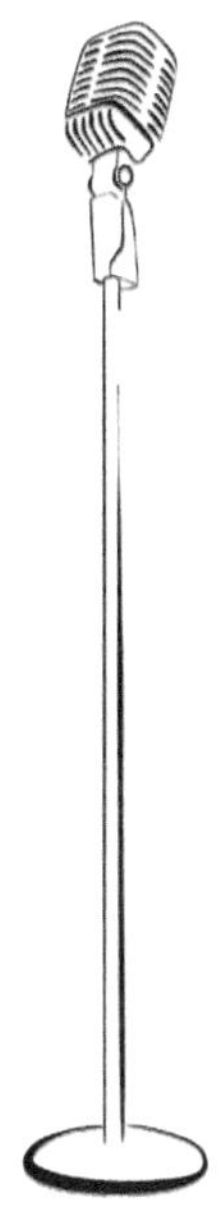

As early as two years of age, he would belt out a tune in the back seat of his mother's car. He grew up listening to all of the classic rock songs of the 80s and as a teenager he would sing his favourite songs in the shower. Frequenting pubs with friends, he would watch any live band, sing along to all the songs, and would dream about one day being the front man of his own band.

He fancies himself a good singer and can belt out a tune as well as the next vocalist.

Answering an advertisement for local talent to join a band, he attends the meeting and excitement sets in. The room is filled with people who play an instrument and have always wanted to join a band. The organiser groups individuals to form several mismatched bands. The newly formed band agree on a name and set off to break into the pub scene.

After weeks of rehearsals and an impressive catalogue of songs, it isn't long before the first gig arrives. The Performer beams a bright white smile and scanning the crowd for the adoring fans he ensures all eyes are on him. He works the crowd like a seasoned professional and they lap up the performance.

He is charismatic on stage and knows how to engage the crowd. He jumps in, dancing and sharing the microphone with willing audience members.

Adoring fans approach him and shower him with the accolades he expects. The attention feeds into his desire to do better and he cannot wait to return to the stage but first a well-deserved couple of beers.

Dancing, singing and cheering, it is clear to see the audience is having a great time. His confidence level is now off the charts. He is even more energised on stage and as the night draws to a close, the crowd wants more and the Performer is only too happy to oblige.

On his way to work he drives past the pub and notices his face on a large billboard. Distracted he almost runs into the car in front of him as he looks twice to check if he actually did see himself. The pub are advertising the band with one of their promotional photos for the upcoming gig.

Smiling to himself, the performer continues on to work knowing that he achieved his dream. He is the front man of a pub band so successful that he drives past himself on billboards.

Always in his blood, he is a performer.

Set goals

Make plans

Chase your dreams – however great or small.

Circus of Narcissism

A narcissist in the workplace can cause irreparable damage to the staff and the organisation. Signs and symptoms to look out for are grandiosity, an exaggerated sense of self-importance, excessive need for admiration, superficial and exploitative relationships, and lack of empathy.

Welcome to the Circus of Narcissism!

She appears to stand grand with a beautiful and shiny marquee, tough on the outside and a crumbling mess on the inside. Smokescreens and mirrors mask the truth – a path of destruction, chaos, and desolation.

The Circus will use illusion to portray an authentic and spectacular performance. To the untrained eye, the audience believe they are in for treat and they sit in awe and lap up the well-rehearsed promise of a performance extraordinaire. Popcorn and soft drink in hand they are ready and waiting.

Let the show begin!

The performance is just that – glam and makeup and looking the part but fails to deliver on the spectacle that was promised.

The audience stand in protest and leave.

The Circus will say the audience should appreciate the effort that was put into the bright, beautiful, and shiny façade. Lack of empathy settles in. The audience will not be granted a full refund as they chose to leave. How dare they leave!

Feelings arise of emptiness, boredom and losing control of a grandiose sense of self.

The Circus feels threatened.

She needs to engage in superficial interactions with other staff members to rebuild the view that she is exceptional. New relationships are created only to inflate her positive self-image.

These new relationships are short lived. The staff grow tired of her entitlement and the endless need to win excessive admiration. In the absence of self-reflection, she happily discards the disobedient and searches for staff who will admire the success, power, beauty and brilliance.

Most have been able to leave the Circus via the exit door, but for some, the exit is not so clear. They become the Circus' safety net, an opportunity to perform with choreographed theatrics and an element of looming danger.

The marketing strategy repeats itself. Exhibitions of pageantry, feats of skill and a small scattering of the slapstick humour of clowns abounds. A travelling performance, wildly disordered. Screaming out for love, applause and adoration from the audience, the

Circus is clever in her approach, conducting research and knowing just how much danger to add to the show to discover who shall return.

The line outside of the marquee has dwindled. Everyone who has attended the Circus has decided that the theatrics are not for them. They have gone. Gone elsewhere. Anywhere but the Circus.

Some do invest in another ticket in the hope that the experience this time will be different, better with well-choreographed awe-inspiring acts and eye-catching costumes. They approach her colourful marquee with anticipation. The audience take their seat and a very familiar smokescreen appears. Once again, the promise of a spectacular show fails to deliver.

Empty seats, empty marquee, and tired looking equipment, obliterated by the constant lack of care and maintenance. The safety net, held together by a few remaining strands.

The Circus declares, 'It's not my fault, it wasn't built strong enough! It should have been unbreakable.'

The Circus moves on to the next town and erects the marquee. Full glam, bright lights and the promise of a spectacular performance. A town crier can be heard for miles: 'Roll up! Roll up!'

A small line starts to build outside of the entrance.

The Sentence

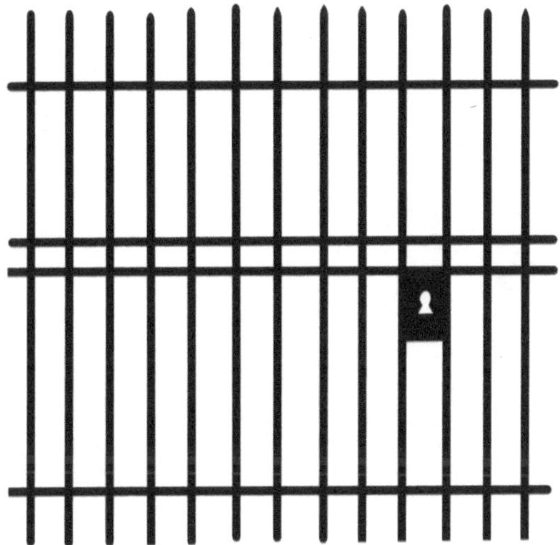

The Sentence is a job where you feel trapped!

You have tried to get out for good behaviour, but the application is denied. You feel you have served your time, yet you have not been acquitted of your sentence.

In the beginning everything is great, light, and fun. You invest an enormous amount of time, and every minute is enjoyable.

Determined to be successful, you take on board all feedback, you learn, and grow. Opportunities for professional development present and you eagerly express interest. Building an impressive skillset you feel ready to progress and patiently wait for the right vacancy.

Years go by and the walls of the jail become all too familiar. Job opportunities have come and gone, but only available to a select few. You have served time, survived despite the broken promises and lies of your manager. But things are different now. The inmate is not the same. She is older and wiser.

Time spent now is hard time, and work becomes a monotonous dreary chore. You must endure the lengthy meetings where workplace discussions are held to develop policies – policies that appear to be fair and equitable for all, but you know the truth.

Feeling trapped, you listen to the hypocrisy. Keeping honest thoughts to yourself, you participate and contribute to the discussion. Any contribution is quickly diminished to a suggestion. Feeling overlooked and undervalued you are sent back to your cell for immediate lock up.

You continue to be professional, show up, do your best and hold onto the hope that liberation is just around the corner. You witness countless job opportunities continually awarded to others. Questioning the appointment with the warden you are met with the monologue – the same monotonous story that has been told many a time before with no end of the Sentence in sight.

You have been sentenced to your role and there you will stay. Not entitled to the same basic rights as others, you must stand up straight and applaud the successful progression of others.

You learn to filter yourself around the other inmates and especially the warden. You are careful with your words, and you watch what you say and how you behave. You have learnt your lessons and have endured the endless punishments that ensue when you slip and forget to filter yourself.

You learn to accept that the Sentence is here to stay, and you do your best to keep the filter in place.

Filtered conversations, filtered outfits, filtered reactions and emotions because solitary confinement is worse than the cell and freedom is nowhere in sight!

SUBURBAN

Newly married, you've just moved into a new home, a new area, and it is all very exciting and fun. The neighbourhood is lively. Everyone is pruning and primping the front lawn and flowerbeds and sweeping the leaves and debris from the curb side. Streetscape appearances are important.

Invitations to regular meetings commence. Not wanting to seem rude, you and your partner attend the first meeting. The small formal lounge room is full of friendly strangers.

Introductions are made and someone is appointed the chair and minute taker. It's all very official for a neighbourly get together but you go along with it, listen and contribute where appropriate. The neighbours are very welcoming if not a little nosy.

Back home, coffee in hand, you and your partner giggle at the bizarre suburban ritual you just participated in.

Life goes on and morning rolls around, ready for the workday to begin. Rubbish is placed in the large bin.

As the lid slams shut, you turn around and notice a ghost-like figure of a woman standing on the inside of the house across the road, looking out from behind the blinds. She is wearing a long white flowing nightgown and an unruly mane of long black wiry hair cascading over her shoulders. You try to adjust your eyes. Is it a ghost?

You soon realise it is your new neighbour. Awkwardly you wave to the neighbour, and she waves back. You get in your car and drive to work, a little bemused by the morning's haunting.

After the workday and a short commute home you pull into the driveway and park the car in the garage. You take a short walk to the mailbox to collect the daily mail. There are some envelopes, bills and advertising catalogues and a handwritten note on a scrappy piece of paper.

Intrigued, you open the note and are surprised to learn that the ghostly neighbour has written to explain the odd circumstances of the morning.

It reads:

> *I thought I would explain what happened this morning. I don't normally stand and stare out my window.*

Ironically, the handwritten note only adds to the odd event that took place earlier in the day.

When your partner comes home from work, you laugh and say, 'You're not going to believe what happened this morning.'

Another drive home and the neighbour is sweeping the leaves in the curb side on a windy day. Pulling into your driveway, you wave hello and smirk to yourself as you try to rationalise why she would do this. With every brush of the broom more leaves fall into the section she has just swept.

Weekends are not spared of the suburban rituals. Saturday, a chance to sleep in, is met with the noise of lawnmowers, leaf blowers and the chatter of neighbours coming together in the street. You join the unofficial meeting taking place and it isn't long before a neighbour sings 'WE HAVE COFFEEEEEE!'

Trying to walk your dog is never a simple task. At least ten different conversations are had with the many neighbours who stop to chat to you.

The rituals of suburbia, enjoyed by some but not all.

If you prefer a little more privacy reconsider moving to the countryside.

LEADERSHIP

There is something to be said about the importance of work, life experience and maturity when it comes to leadership. Organisations try to create leaders from people who are good at their jobs, but being good at your job doesn't necessarily translate to being a good leader. Leadership requires an array of skills, but one of the most important is knowing how to lead with integrity.

Staff need to feel that they are trusted to perform their role. They also need to know that when times are tough, they will be supported. Micromanaging someone is an express train to stifling their enthusiasm.

Destination?

Resignation!

Another station along the same route is the leader who does not know what their staff do. They ask the staff how things are done and place unrealistic demands on them. There is a disconnect between what the staff does and what the manager thinks they ought to be doing.

Or the manager who is appointed because they were in the right place at the right time. They put their hand up, interested in the title and salary regardless of experience or interest in the role.

The delegator is an interesting leader. They appear to be achieving great heights but if you were to unpack this type, often you will find a team of people who have been working tirelessly until all hours of the night.

The manager attends the important meetings and discusses all their wonderful achievements without a single thought or care for the team who deserve the acknowledgment.

Toot! Toot! The sound of their own horn, so too the sound of the train pulling up to resignation.

People who feel appreciated will always do more than what is expected. Appreciate your team and what they bring to the table.

TEAM stands for Together Everyone Achieves More.

The title manager does not elevate anyone to a level where you are not to be spoken to, or that you should see anyone else as subordinate.

The best kind is someone who is experienced, knowledgeable and treats everyone with kindness and respect regardless of their position.

Be a leader that everyone wants to follow.

Golden Fare

He parks so close, almost inside the building. To walk any distance would be too much. His hips, knees and ankles would not cope with the mere thought of even the slowest of paces. His heart cannot take the rush of oxygen pumping through the veins. No! No extra steps will be taken.

Each stride seems unimaginable, torturous, but he pushes through, huffing and puffing until he reaches the door, and then his office. He stops to catch his breath, then takes a seat.

He is on top of his throne, on top of the world, and he's now in control. He can reach all that he needs to get through the day, the keyboard and phone at arm's length.

Lunchtime ticks over and the thought of food overpowers everything. Up and out of the throne, he embarks on the trek to the fish'n'chip store.

The distance is greater than to the car, yet somehow it is manageable, if not enjoyable, as there is a pot of gold at the end of this trail – golden deep-fried fish in batter, chips, dim sims, and potato cakes all laced with white powder, otherwise known as sodium chloride or, simply, salt. The walk back takes no time at all, the excitement of tearing open the package too much to bear.

The package of gold is placed reverently on the table. Now the chair puzzle ensues: a chair here and a chair there. Only certain chairs will participate in the gastronomic event.

Everything in its place, his fingers tear open the white paper encasing the golden fare. More sodium chloride is sprinkled to each treasure exposed within the neatly folded paper package, as well as a little on the table too. Red lashings of tomato sauce adorn the golden delights like tinsel on a Christmas tree. The feast is washed down by buckets of cola.

The scene is set for the main event: the ingestion. Forks and knives are not required. Fingers are the in-built cutlery. They ravage the golden fare, catapulting flecks of crispy goodness through the air, across the table and onto unsuspecting neighbouring staff.

Liquid gold drips from each bite and oozes down the digits and onto the table. With each wipe, the remaining oil is collected and saved in the fabric of his pants.

Lunchtime feasts alternate between hamburgers, lamb korma, pizza with the lot, fried chicken, and fish and chips. This occasional treat for some is the daily staple for him. Attempts to redirect and guide his eating habits to a healthier lifestyle fall flat.

The 3.00pm munchies call with food delivered to

your door for a price. The walk to the store is no longer required. A brown paper bag housing a freshly baked chocolate éclair is washed down by a large caffeine-laden beveridge. All is well for the rest of the day. Chocolate éclair today, a croissant tomorrow and an iced cupcake the next.

The others exhale as the need to perform CPR was not necessary today, but they keep emergency services on speed dial just in case.

The strength, stamina and determination to purchase Golden Fare overpowers the awareness, will, and commonsense to prioritise his health.

Flames

There have been years of tears and blaming anyone and everyone but himself. Daily calls from school to collect his daughter as her behaviour can no longer be tolerated. The anger builds while the ability to rationalise dissipates.

He builds a case against the system and collects a team, his army, to give him the courage and strength to stand tall and roar fire from the summit of his mountain.

His fire scorches all it touches. Over time he burns all the help, resources and support and networks and he starts to implode – the fire that started as an ember in the sanctuary of home.

One shiny bright spark and one with a dim light that constantly flickers, with multiple challenges. The ideal is shattered and reality of what is has set in. He doesn't like it.

Unhappy and angry, he searches for refuge from his own being – a refuge that cannot be found in anything other than the bottom of a bottle. He wishes he was anyone but himself. He occupies the human form of a demon, a tormentor on earth.

Unable to see his own reflection, or the ability to self-reflect, the only option is to turn the mirror onto everyone else.

Their fault that behaviour is escalating, their fault that friendships are not forming, their fault that learning is not happening, their fault, their fault, their fault.

Always.

Some have tried to extinguish the flames and offer hope but he has come to find comfort in the familiarity of the firepit. It is his home and anything else would seem foreign. He would lose control. Lose the right to feel entitled to treat everyone else badly.

Supports now scorched and scarred, exhausted, they no longer want to play with the fire. They realise that no amount of support will ever be enough to protect them from the flames. They move on and treat the burns.

What remains is the same angry demon, perched at the summit of the mountain, throwing flames in all directions. No amount of firefighters or extinguishers could ever be enough.

He is forever scorched.

Married/Single?

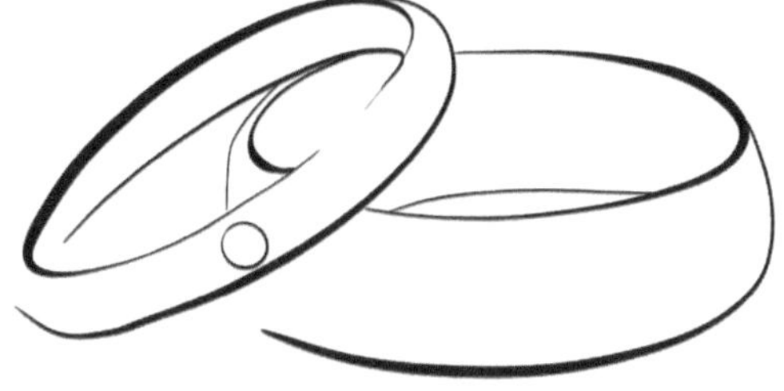

He has built a successful business and enjoys the finer things in life. Married at a young age, he has four beautiful children. His home, in an affluent suburb, is designed to meet his specifications. The garage is a sacred place that securely houses his much-loved cars. He has one for the working week and an incredibly fast sports car for fun on the weekends.

Working long hours, he retreats to his home theatre. There he sits for hours with the largest television screen that money can buy watching Formula 1 and action movies. He sinks more than just a few glasses of his favourite aged scotch until falling into bed. He has not a single thought for his wife who has also worked a long day, prepared dinner, cleaned the mess, bathed the children, and tucked them into bed.

The weekends are his to enjoy. Upon rising he spends hours at the gym, alternating between working his arms and legs. All the while his wife is dressing the children and preparing breakfast. She chauffeurs them to and from playdates while he takes his sports car out for a long and fast drive.

Annual family holidays are always the same: his wife and children are occupied with family friendly activities as he sets off on individual adventures – scuba diving, surfing the waves, Formula 1 racetrack rides, skydiving and rock climbing.

Occasionally, he joins the family for dinner. Hiring a convertible sportscar, he cruises along the coastline and stops at the sites along the way, enjoying the views and a local pinot noir.

Back home and it's not too long before he returns to his routine. Cruising on a Sunday afternoon, the speedometer is raging out of control and he doesn't see the barrier that he clips with the front of the car. He does feel the car become airborne. It flies across three lanes, just missing oncoming traffic. The tyres screech to a halt as the car collides with the brick barrier wall on the other side of the freeway.

In hospital he nurses bruises and broken bones, but he is alive. He has a lot of time to think. The best part of his day is when the children come to visit. Loud, noisy, laughter and lots of cuddles and a sneaky kiss or two from his wife. The realisation of what is most important is finally realised. When they leave, the silence is overwhelming and he can't wait to be home surrounded by the chaos.

Well enough he arrives home and with arms wide open he scoops up his children. He doesn't even feel the tinges of pain as the hugs press on his bruises.

A married man with children only now he knows it.

Marionette

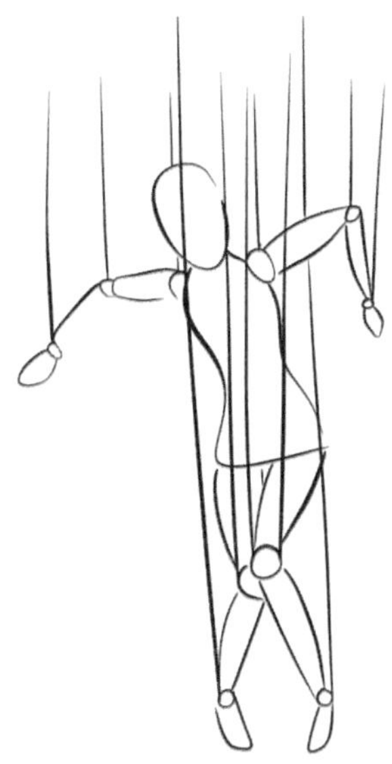

A grown woman, she has lived her whole life being told what to do, how to live, who to see and who to be. She takes in all advice and continues to live in a world where others pull the strings. For years, it was her parents and friends.

She was too polite to challenge this.

Highly intelligent she would easily fly through any degree, masters or doctorate but opts for a simpler life. She works a nine-to-five office job with flexi time and lives humbly with her beloved feline friend. Never married, she spends hours in her studio painting.

Boyfriends have come and gone but none have passed the test of the Matriarch.

Until now.

The new boyfriend is younger, handsome and makes her laugh. Divorced with no children.

At first, he immerses himself in her world and all is well for years … until it isn't. There one minute and gone the next. Not from her life, just her world. No longer does he attend functions, gatherings, or any typical ritual.

He has taken full control of the strings and pulls them in all directions that lead back to him. Her time is now devoted to ensuring that he is happy, fed and entertained.

She is no longer spending time in her studio and even her much-loved cat misses her. She is now living for the puppet master. With a firm grip of the reins, he demands to know where she is at all times. She rarely sees her family and friends and has reduced her working hours.

When with him, she must solely devote all of her attention to him. She cannot spend time with anyone else, call anyone else or do anything else. When he works, she will clean his house, stock his pantry, collect his dry cleaning, walk his dog, prepare the evening meal, and makes sure that she punctually picks him up at the end of the day and takes him home.

On the weekends, she must spend every waking minute with him.

When he has finally had enough, she is allowed to go home for free time. She can now shower her cat with affection and spend some quality time in her studio, but it isn't long before the phone rings and the Marionette has been redirected back to him.

Her friends and family have observed the all-consuming, string pulling of the puppet master and have tried to inch scissors close enough to set her free.

But he is fast and yanks her back to him.

ANGEL

Bright eyed and a perfect smile, she is full of life. Taking pride in all that she does she finds joy in the most mundane of daily chores. Everyone who meets her is drawn into her warm and genuine persona. She is chatty, loud, and has an infectious laugh.

Working in customer service she takes her role seriously, remembering details of her customers and wishing all a great day. Going out of her way to do her absolute best, her line is always the longest. People are happy to wait longer to be served by her.

Her practical and easy-going approach to life makes her even more endearing. She is the rock of her family and is a never-ending source of love and support.

Her happy place? A spot on her favourite beach. Days spent laying in the sun followed by endless sunsets with shades of orange, red and yellow fill the sky. Basking in the glow of the sun and wrapped in the warmth of love from her family, she feels blessed.

A natural in the kitchen, her culinary skills are a work of art. She prepares, cooks, presents and serves food like a seasoned chef. If you are one of the lucky ones you are in for a real treat.

Struck by a terminal illness, it isn't long before she succumbs to the diagnosis.

Enormous waves of grief wash over everyone who knew her. Overwhelming sadness is now the glue that binds those that remain.

Appreciate people who are kind and genuine. Here today but they may not be tomorrow. All that remains are memories.

Make

    Every

        Moment

            Count!

Sadly missed but never forgotten.

Zero

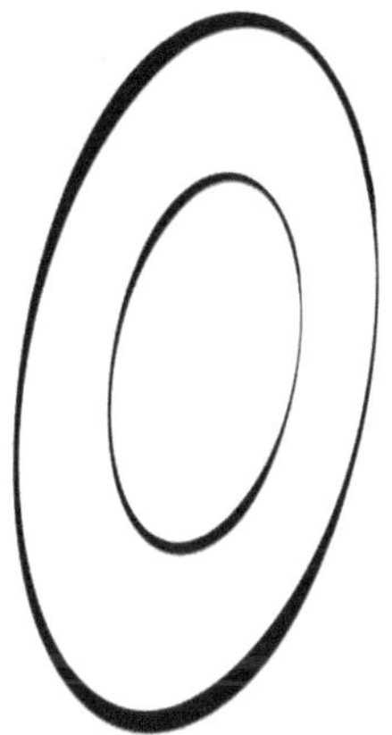

Attending an exclusive private school, he is in his final year and does not want to be there. On the edge of 18, another world awaits: work, driving, gym workouts and socialising – all uniform free. Another full year of school is too much to bear.

The school year begins, and each day is a battle. First class for the day and the teacher marks his absence. So it goes until the odd day that he graces a random class with his presence. He is not in full uniform, as this would be conforming. That is not what he wants to be.

The teacher requests that he stays back at the end of class to discuss how much he has missed and a potential plan for him to catch up. He has a conversation with the teacher and goes home agitated. He tells his parents that he has been bullied by his teacher. The following day he does not attend school in protest.

His parents ring the school to complain that the teacher has bullied their son. They will not stand for it, and he will not be back until the teacher mends their ways. The teacher is shocked as he asked the student to complete the task that was asked of all students. This was the bullying in reference.

His attendance for the year is sprinkled like confetti, a little bit over here and a little bit over there, but there remains not a completed task in sight. He has done nothing.

Zero.

End of year rolls around and final reports and conversations take place. The meeting is tense and serious. The teachers are drained from coddling Zero through the year.

Mum and Dad, disappointed, contribute little and as the meeting comes to an end, Dad thanks the staff for not giving up.

A small win! A little acknowledgment for a years' worth of effort. Zero could not be happier: no more school in sight. He can wear the fashion of choice, track pants and make a plan to get a job.

Just not yet!

First is the fun to be had over the summer – driving, socialising, sleeping in and doing lots of nothing.

Doing zero!

GOAT HERDER

The only son of migrant parents, he lives in a modest home with his elderly parents on acres of prime land. The area has changed greatly over the years with multimillion dollar homes now surrounding their farm. Real estate agents doorknock frequently to encourage the family to place the farm on the market. It is a property developers goldmine!

They share the land with hundreds of sheep, goats, and cows. He spends his day tending to the animals and herds them from his property to the vacant land across the road to graze on the overgrown grass and back again.

His parents tend to the vegetables and eat a clean diet. His role is to care for the animals and he takes this role seriously. A teenage ewe gives birth to a lamb and rejects it. She is not ready to be a mama sheep and she stops feeding her. The lamb is losing strength and her health declines.

Not wanting to leave the lamb unattended, he sleeps in the barn and ensures she is kept safe and warm. When the morning light shines through the window, he opens his eyes and is happy that the lamb made it through the night.

Remembering a neighbour not too far has a sheep who recently had twin lambs he drives to the neighbour's property. The lamb sleeps in his arms as he drives.

When he arrives, he steps out of the car with the frail lamb in his arms. An overwhelming aroma of musty barnyard animals wafts out of the car like a big fluffy cloud and slowly floats away, dissipating. The neighbour's sheep feeds the ailing lamb until she has grown.

The Goat Herder continues to care for his animals on a small hobby farm, living off the land with his mother and father all the while million-dollar homes continue to be built around him.

The sound of opportunistic agents knocking on his door is drowned out by the bleating, mooing and baaing of the most cared for farm animals.

ROTTEN APPLE

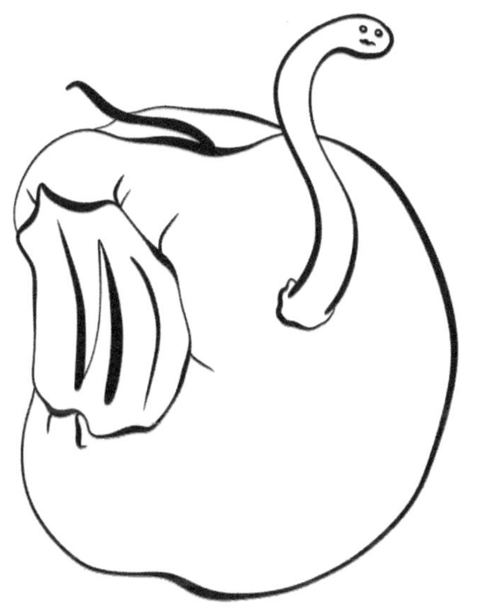

Having been there for just a few months, she feels entitled, even though it's her first-ever job. She is angry that her friend was not employed in the same team. Expressing this in the only way she knows how, she will not say a word to the successful incumbent and ensures her voice is heard by speaking to and *through* the other staff.

Not one positive word to say, she spends her time speaking poorly of others and undermining new initiatives. Uncomfortable with her demeaner the others try to disassociate but often feel unable to exit. Some indulge in the behaviour and before long a toxic environment is created.

Oblivious to the effect she has on others, she approaches each day with arrogance and a know-it-all attitude. Her colleagues grow increasingly frustrated with the constant lack of humility. Management schedule endless meetings and provide professional development opportunities which are always met with the same response: 'What a waste of time. I already know this.'

Lacking emotional intelligence, she provides an array of excuses for her behaviour. Unable to reflect on the feedback provided she points the finger of blame in every direction except her own.

She is provided with a plan forward and agrees to be present and participate in meetings, training, social events and is supported by weekly debrief sessions with a supervisor. But it isn't long before her old ways resurface.

Taking lengthy lunches and casually strolling in without a care in the world, she sits at the table surrounded by at least fifteen others. Late by ten minutes, not a notebook in sight, phone in hand, she is distracted. Laughing to herself, she responds to the text message, knowing full well that she is seen.

Absenteeism becomes a regular and predictable pattern, so much so that management has lost track of how many days she has missed.

The weather heats up and so does her social invitations. Work now gets in the way of her life – any excuse to leave early and join her friends.

Other staff have expressed concern that her absence is impacting the workload for them. They are tired, overworked and feel it is unfair. Another sick day and it is the final straw. She is called into the manager's office and within a half hour her locker is emptied.

She does not return
Gone!
Supporting the bad seed was an ongoing and exhaustive process, which affected the whole team.

A slow and steady process but before long the team camaraderie has improved.

Rotten Apple is a bad seed who contaminated the soil and infected everybody.

Now that she is gone, the soil is clean, the air is clear, and everybody feels like they can grow again.

THE PROCESS

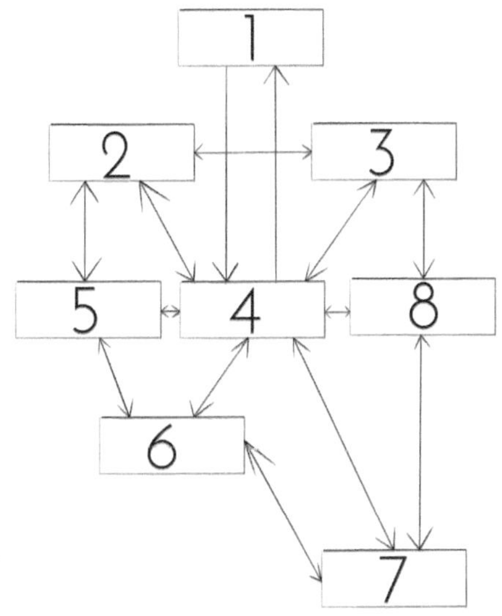

All organisations and companies have a Human Resources department of sorts. They have their own guidelines and processes that govern how they run the organisation and manage its people.

When a position is created or vacated it is advertised on the intranet site and on external platforms. It would seem they are trying to operate by an open and transparent process. Often this is the guise to recruit a person of choice.

It is evident when the successful candidate is announced that they were always going to be the successful candidate. Little signs give this away. Roles advertised for a short period often indicate that they already have someone in mind but are simply going through the process to appear to be operating in a fair and equitable manner.

The Process is interesting. An application is required by internal and external candidates – a letter of application, a statement of key selection criteria and a current copy of your resumé. In order to even be considered for the interview you must address each of the listed dot points in the key selection criteria.

Naturally you assume this means that they really are wanting to recruit the best fit for the role. But then comes the official announcement of the successful applicant. They are a friend of one of the senior staff and it becomes abundantly clear that although you addressed all of the key selection criteria dot points, you were never really in with a chance because the friend was always going to be appointed.

The recruitment process is just a red herring for organisations to continue to do as they please.

The Ewe

She is no longer a lamb, but her wardrobe does not know this. She has always used her assets to get ahead and continues to do so. It has worked for her all these years.

Happy to wear outfits that display too much, she positions herself in the prime spot to ensure maximum exposure to the right people. This has certainly helped her career progression.

Everyone else would need to actually meet a selection criteria. She doesn't hide the fact that she has no qualifications. She has been in the right place at the right time.

Hmmm.

She is strategic in her approach. She knows how to deliver and impress the powers that be. She delegates tasks to the staff she supervises.

Delivering a comprehensive verbal list to each staff member in her team, she feels a sense of achievement knowing that they will complete all tasks.

Out of the corner of her eye through a perfectly attached lash she sees one of the managers. She sashays away from the team who are working hard and calls after the manager, using her sweetest voice like the call of a siren.

At times the staff are unsure how to achieve a deliverable and ask the Ewe for guidance. She has no clue. She will direct the staff to either ask other staff or to look at the archived files to work out how to complete the tasks.

With the team doing all of the work, the ewe ensures she is dressed to impress and delivers the information to ensure her position is secure.

Look at me and all I have achieved! Look at me! Everybody, look at me!

If a position is vacant in her team, it doesn't matter if you meet the selection criteria. If you are younger and prettier you need not apply. You don't stand a chance!

You will not take away the attention from the Ewe, even unintentionally.

THE ROCK

Everyone needs a Rock to lean on.

As a young child I always looked up to mine.

They were always there, supporting and guiding me. I recall looking up to them in awe. They are older, beautiful and sensible. A great sense of humour and hearts of gold, never knowing how much their beauty transcended all around them. They never saw themselves this way.

Ever the voice of reason they embodied all I could ever want to be as an adult. I trust them both with my life. They are my collaborators, co-conspirators and role models.

They have allowed me to make mistakes and learn from them and are my go-to for all things life related. Voices of reason and love that never wavers. They are non judgmental and have my back no matter what.

They have listened to the countless stories and associated hurt that has come from previous chapters, such as Red Flags, Wounded and the Leech, and have provided some much-needed advice. They offer guidance around conflict resolution in friendships and when to walk away.

We share the same sense of humour that no one else seems to understand. Once we start laughing, it is impossible to try and stop us. We can communicate with simply a look, and we know what the other one is thinking. At times saying just one word is enough to set us off.

For all the chapters, I am grateful for this one! They are the longest relationships in my life with shared upbringing, genes and secrets.

We are connected by an eternal bond.

Sisters, always connected by the heart.

They are my rock.

SSSSNAKE
IN THE STAFF ROOM

L unchtime in the staff room, the sandwich press getting quite the workout with copious cups of coffee and tea being poured. Staff settle into the same seats as the day before, and the day before that. Creatures of habit they don't even notice the ritual.

A number of casual conversations take place – you would be mistaken to think it was a room full of friends. Some are genuinely human, but some are serpents.

They are in disguise, eating a toasted sandwich and sipping on cups of tea. They are clever, cold blooded and form alliances with all the right people.

A serpent will have you believe that you are just having a conversation, but their questions are loaded. Listening intently, they take notes, filing them away in their head, saving them for a later day.

A casual conversation around a possible transfer within the team and the closest Ssssnake with a photographic memory takes snapshots of all the details and asks all the right questions. A week later and the announcement is made in a team meeting –

Ssssnake is appointed the transfer.

They are guarded too! They ask numerous questions about you, your job, your life and never divulge anything personal about themselves – except when it's time to compare to others. They always state that they know it all and do everything better. An upcoming holiday and the Ssssnake will say they have been there but their holiday was better.

Where they live is better.

What they wear is better.

How they cook is better.

And the list goes on.

The Ssssnakes need to do this, to build themselves up, placing themselves on a pedestal built of the pieces of flesh bitten off others.

Endeavouring to engage in a conversation will leave you a little dumbfounded. It doesn't take long before reality sets in. You have been bitten by a snake.

If you see a Ssssnake the warnings are the same for all. Be incredibly still and it will slither over your feet to the next moving target.

Genuine

It has been a month since the last coffee and chat and there is so much to say. Big hugs and smiles to see a friendly face. Meeting at the same café.

The same coffee order.

And now the fight for airtime. The friends talk over each other about all-things-life with gusto. Taking a breath, they stop and laugh. At times the laughter is so infectious – neighbouring patrons cannot help but smile.

The café owner collects the empty mugs and before he can walk away the friends say, 'Another round please.'

They barely notice that hours have passed, and other patrons have come and gone.

No judgement. Just easy and fun.

Conversations are free flowing without fear or favour. No greater feeling than being able to be yourself.

Unfiltered.

Achievements are celebrated with another caffeinated Beveridge. And, sometimes, a slice of something sweet.

Another round? Asks the café owner.

Contemplating for just a moment – they look at the time and realise the catch up has come to an end.

Back to life they go.

Until the next month.

Treasure these friendships.

For some they are a quick get together and for others they are lifeline.

DREAMER

She is an attractive blonde and she knows it. She has always used her looks to get what she wants. Living off the income that her brother provides, she affords designer clothing, tattoos, cars, and anything else that her heart desires.

Without a care in the world, she does not know or care to know *how* her brother earns a living that provides a bountiful life for them both.

No need to get a job, she is more than happy to live this easy and comfortable life. Men come and go and it is not long before she finds she is expecting – twins. The babies' father sticks around during the pregnancy. And it is at this time that her brother disappears. For work perhaps? She doesn't mind. Its not about her love for him but his money.

She spends numerous hours visiting her family and friends disclosing every last detail about the expensive car she intends to buy, her move to an exclusive seaside town, and how she will only feed her unborn babies the most organic diet. Her ideal lifestyle story sounds more and more like a fairy-tale with each detail.

But with newborn twins to care for, she is overwhelmed by the enormity of the task. The babies' father provides some financial stability but she feels trapped by the enormous task of caring for them.

She dreams of a better lifestyle, of glamming it up, dressing in designer labels and frequenting exclusive events. She spends days changing nappies, bathing the babies, feeding the babies, and trying to establish a sleep routine all while wearing sweatpants.

Wanting a little bit of fun she drops off her babies to her mother's house. Feeling great in evening wear and a full face of makeup she states, 'I won't be too late.'

Her mother feeds and bathes the babies and settles them down for a sleep. The clock ticks over early into the morning and her mother goes to bed. Her daughter doesn't return until late Sunday to collect the babies.

With her mother nearby to provide convenient babysitting, her planned move to the exclusive seaside town never eventuates. Neither does the new car, organic diet, and anything else that she has said in such great detail.

She continues to visit her friends and talk about this exclusive life that she intends to have. They all listen patiently to the same story retold while flicking the switch on the kettle and making yet another cup of instant coffee.

Uniquely You

I magine how bland the world would be without all the characters we meet along the way. Some will be in your life for a short period of time while others will stay longer.

These characters will provide some challenges, as well as trying and fun times, but they will all provide the opportunity to learn and grow. A multitude of behaviours are on display to be observed and studied.

A University of Life.

Each character leaves a memory. Battle scars are a constant reminder. Lessons are learned. What is highlighted is that no two people are the same.

The importance now shifts to you and what you do with these lessons and how they affect you.

Do not be afraid to go through the challenging times as they will provide you with many opportunities to learn and grow.

Each experience is a perfect lived demonstration of how *to* and *not* to behave, and how to treat others.

Through it all what is important is that you remain true to yourself.

You are uniquely YOU.

About the Author

She was always drawn to the written word. In school, English was a subject that required no revision. It just came easy. It was enjoyable.

Now, a little bit older, a little bit wiser, and with time on her hands thanks to lengthy lockdowns, she has gone back to writing. She loves to read and to tell a great story.

Collecting stories in one place seemed to be the next logical step. So many experiences: wonderful, happy, sad, bad, and unhealthy.

So many that demanded to be told.

And here they are.

She hopes the reader will connect with a character or two. Or simply enjoy the journey.

A hard worker and loyal friend.

Values instilled in her by her family.

She is the Author.